D0308712

For Joseph Francis Inns

MYRIAD BOOKS LIMITED
35 Bishopsthorpe Road, London SE26 4PA

First published in 2005 by
FRANCES LINCOLN LIMITED
4 Torriano Mews
Torriano Avenue
London NW5 2RZ

The Jokers copyright © Frances Lincoln 2005
Text and illustrations © copyright Chris Inns 2005

Chris Inns has asserted his right to be identified as the
author and illustrator of this work in accordance with
the Copyright, Designs and Patents Act, 1988.

All rights reserved. No part of this publication may be reproduced,
stored in a retrieval system, or transmitted, in any form or by any means
electronic, mechanical, photocopying or otherwise, without the
prior permission of the copyright owner.

ISBN 1 84746 029 1
EAN 9 781 84746 029 5

Printed in China

The Jokers

by Chris Inns

MYRIAD BOOKS LIMITED

Mungo the Elephant and Mr Thunderpants
loved playing jokes on each other...

and they loved playing jokes
on their friends.

They hid clockwork chattering teeth in Dawg's pants,

painted glasses and a moustache on Mrs Moody while she was napping,

used a whoopee cushion in Davey Duck's nest,

put itching powder
in Big Bear's cave,

I'll get those
cheeky monkeys!

left trick blue soap
in Lily's bathroom,

Hurrumph!

Sssave me!

and even put sneezing
powder into Mr Legg's
hat. He sneezed so
much he tied himself
into a knot!

But their friends
didn't always find
the jokes so funny.

One day their friend Lily came to ask them to her dressing-up party. Lily said there was going to be a prize for the silliest costume.

Mungo &
Mr Thunderpants
please come to
my party
from Lily x

Lily said she was going as a pirate queen...

Big Bear was going to be a fire-fighter.

Nee Nar! Nee Nar!

Mrs Moody was going to

Davey had decided to be a diver.

Glub! Glub!

Dawg was going as a spaceman.

I grant you three wishes.

The beagle has landed.

ppear as a fairy godmother,

and Mr Legg was going as a cowboy.

Yee Haa!

BANG

ssstick 'em up!

Mungo and Mr Thunderpants imagined how their friends would look in their funny costumes.

Lily hoped they would make an effort
with their costumes.

Mungo and Mr Thunderpants decided that they would make themselves the best costumes ever and win the prize.

They worked hard all afternoon so that their costumes would be ready in time for the party.

They measured,

and cut,

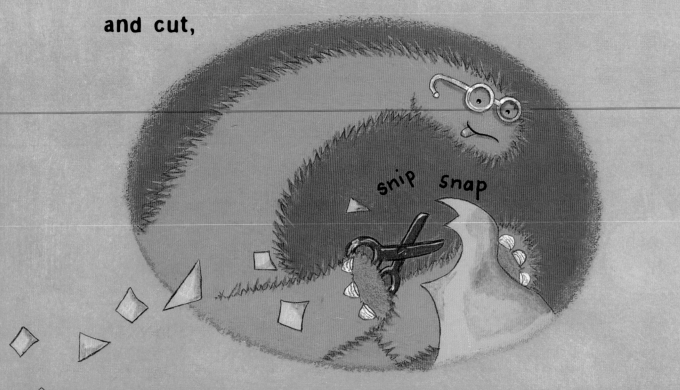

and glued,

and stitched,

until, at last, their costumes were finished.

They quickly got dressed...

When they got to Lily's house
they burst in through the door.

But the surprise...

was on them!

No one else was wearing a costume. It was a joke.
Their friends had got their own back.
Everybody laughed – even
the two jokers!

The party was the best ever – with dancing, games and fantastic party bags. Mungo and Mr Thunderpants clowned around and made everybody laugh.

And they promised not to play any more naughty jokes on their friends...

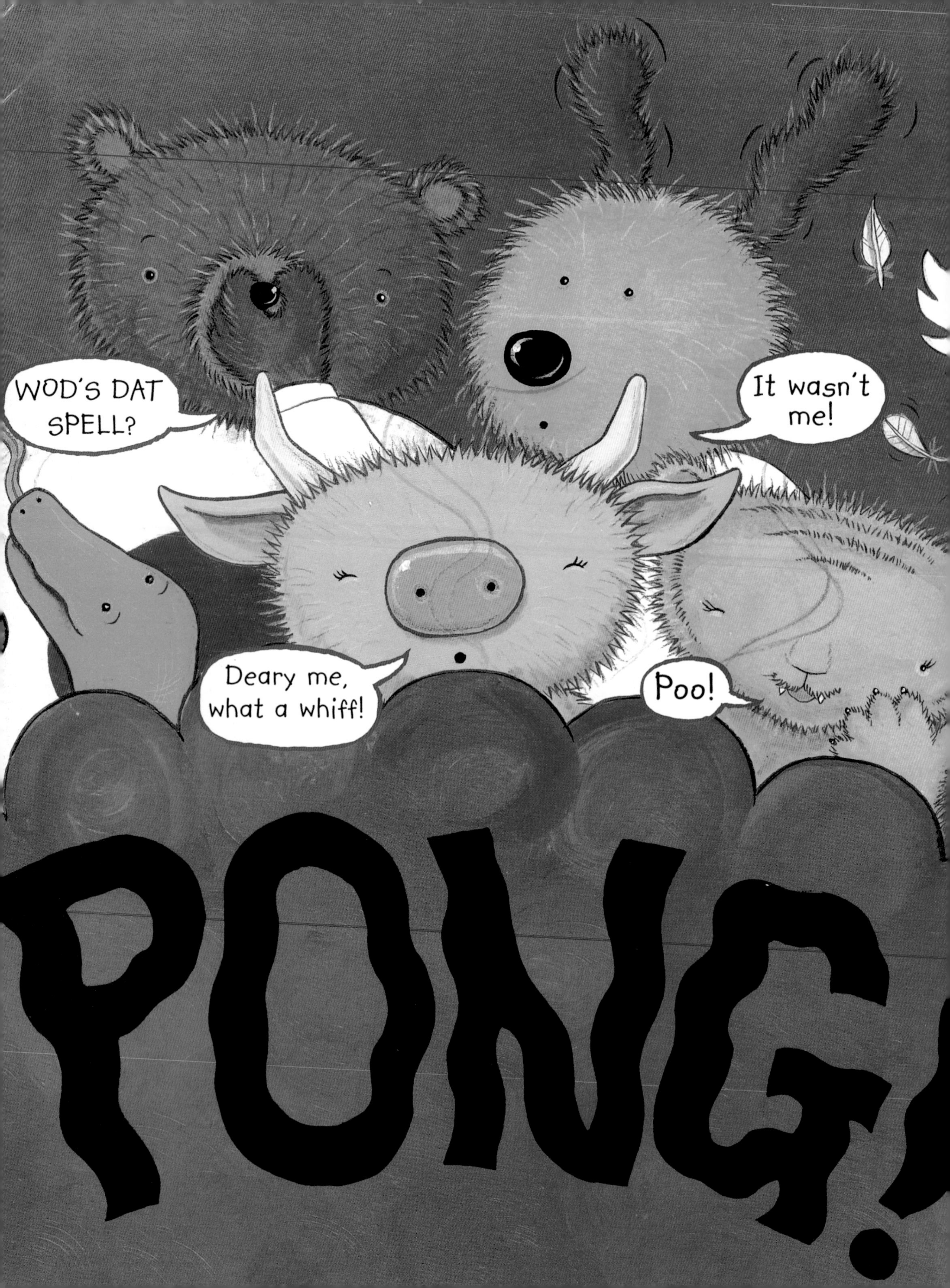
WOD'S DAT SPELL?
It wasn't me!
Deary me, what a whiff!
Poo!
PONG!

MOST of the time!

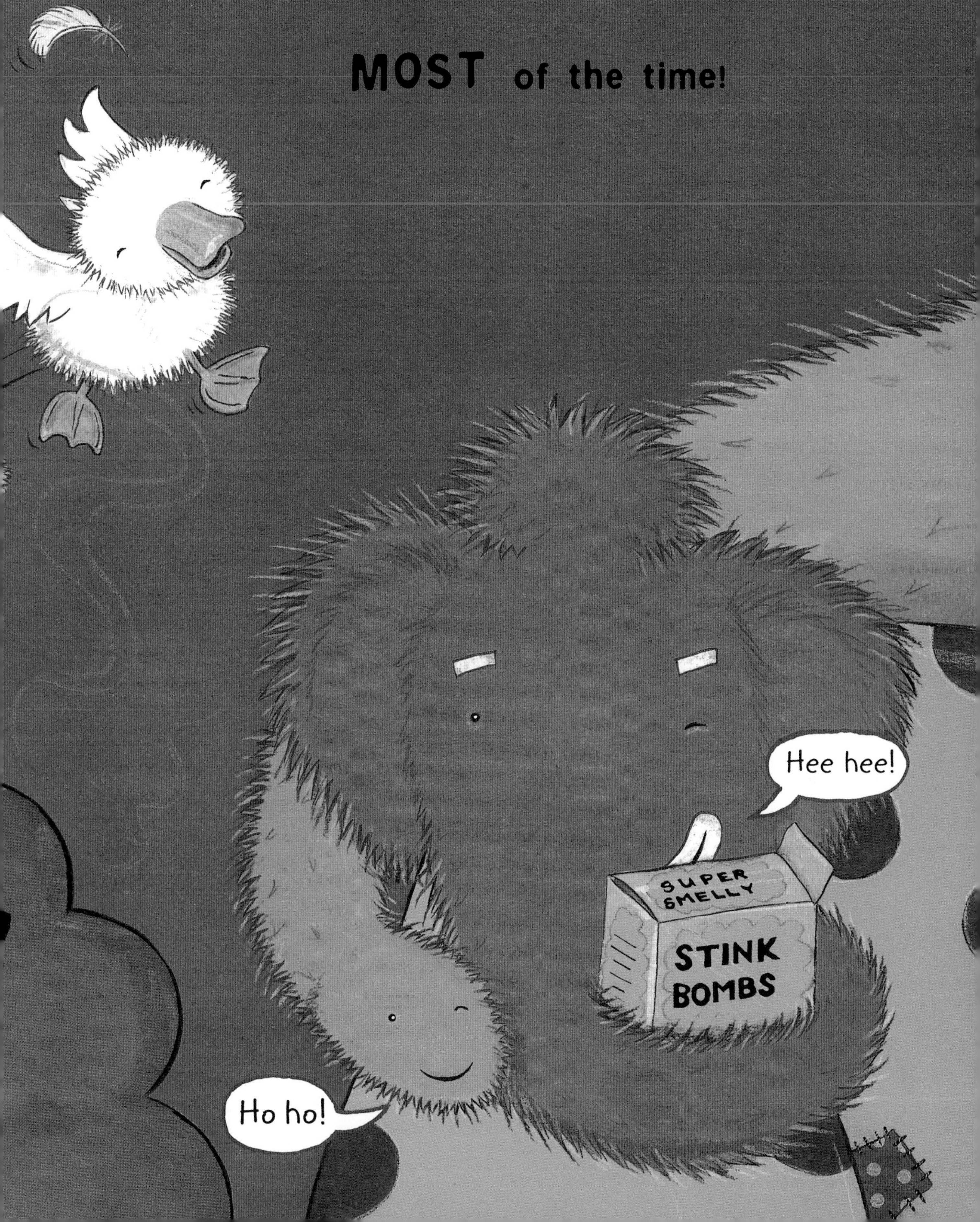